PIZZA FU

Judy Bastyra

For my mother, with love—J.B.

KINGFISHER

Larousse Kingfisher Chambers Inc.
80 Maiden Lane
New York, New York 10038
www.kingfisherpub.com

First published in 1997
4 6 8 10 9 7 5 3

1SCH/0701/TWP/–(CS)/150ARM

LIBRARY OF CONGRESS CATALOGING-IN-PUBLICATION DATA
Bastyra, Judy.
Pizza fun / Judy Bastyra.
p. cm.
Summary: Provides simple recipes for making dough and sauce
with direction for some creative variations.
1. Pizza—Juvenile literature.   [1. Pizza. 2. Cookery.]
I. Title.
TX770.P58838   1997
641.8'24—dc20 96-30161 CIP AC

ISBN 0-7534-5061-5

Editor: Sue Nicholson
Designer: Smiljka Surla
Art editor: Christina Fraser
Photography: Michael Michaels
Illustrations: Julie Beech

Printed in Singapore

Contents

Introduction

This little pizza cookbook will show you how to make lots of different pizzas from just one simple recipe. You'll find the recipe for pizza dough and a tomato sauce topping on pages 6–9. The rest of the pizzas use the same dough and sauce with simple variations. I hope you have as much fun making them as I have!

Judy Bastyra

Little Cook's Rules

Here are some important things to remember:

- Wash your hands before you start to cook, and wear an apron.
- Before you begin, read through the recipe to make sure you have everything you need.
- Always ask an adult to help you when you see this sign:
- Always use oven mitts when handling something hot.
- Turn on the oven 15 minutes before you need it, and remember to turn it off when you have finished cooking.
- Don't forget to clean up!

Little Cook's Tools

Shaped cookie cutters

You will find a list of all the ingredients you need in a box next to each recipe. You will also need:

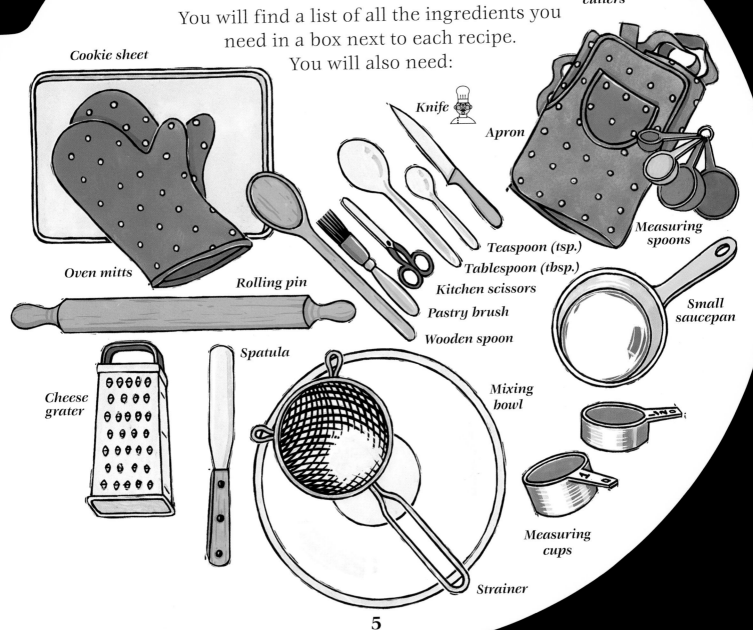

Cookie sheet

Oven mitts

Rolling pin

Knife

Apron

Teaspoon (tsp.)

Tablespoon (tbsp.)

Kitchen scissors

Pastry brush

Wooden spoon

Measuring spoons

Small saucepan

Spatula

Cheese grater

Mixing bowl

Measuring cups

Strainer

Cheese and Tomato Pizza

Once you know how to make this traditional pizza you can easily make all the other pizzas in the book!

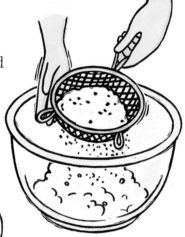

Makes two 8-inch pizzas

1 Sift the flour and salt into a large mixing bowl.

2 Add the yeast, oil, and hot water. Mix into a dough with your fingers.

Pizza Dough Ingredients*

- 2 cups all-purpose flour, plus a little more for kneading and rolling out
- 1 tsp. salt
- 2 tsps. easy-blend dried yeast
- 2 tbsps. olive oil, plus 1 tsp. for greasing the bowl
- 1 cup hot water

3 Sprinkle some flour on your work surface and knead the dough for five minutes.

* It's a good idea to make a lot of dough at the same time. You can store the extra dough in the freezer.

4 Wash, dry, and grease a bowl. Put the dough into the bowl, cover it, and leave it in a warm place for one hour until the dough has risen.

Unrisen dough

Dough after one hour

Stir from time to time

Makes sauce for two pizzas*

Tomato Sauce Ingredients

- 2 tbsps. olive oil
- 1 small onion, chopped
- 2 tbsps. tomato paste
- 1 x 16-oz. can chopped tomatoes, drained
- 1 tsp. dried oregano or basil
- ½ tsp. sugar
- ½ tsp. salt
- pinch of ground black pepper

5 Meanwhile, make the tomato sauce. Heat the oil in a saucepan, add the onion, and cook for 5 minutes.

6 Add the tomato paste, canned tomatoes, herbs, sugar, salt, and pepper and cook for 15 minutes. Cool before using.

* Store any unused sauce in a screw-top jar in the refrigerator for up to a week.

7

7 Divide the dough into two balls. Sprinkle your work surface with flour and roll out the dough.

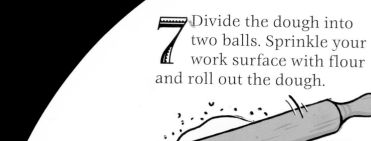

Heat the oven to 375° F and grease two cookie sheets.

Pizza should be about 8 inches wide

8 Place the pizzas on the cookie sheets, brush with olive oil, then add the tomato sauce and grated cheese. Decorate with sliced tomato, Mozzarella, and olives.

Topping Ingredients

- 3 tbsps. grated Cheddar cheese
- 1 tomato, sliced
- 1 small fresh Mozzarella cheese, sliced
- 9 or 10 pitted black olives
- fresh basil leaves

9 Put the pizzas in the oven and bake for 15–20 minutes.

10 Allow the pizzas to cool slightly, then take them off the cookie sheets with a spatula and cut them into wedges.

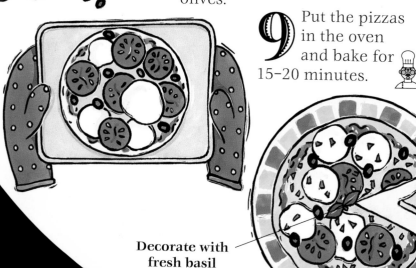

Decorate with fresh basil

Galaxy Pizzas

These small pizzas are great for parties or for a picnic.

1 Divide the dough into three equal balls and roll out three small pizzas.

Brush with olive oil

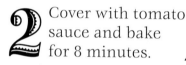

2 Cover with tomato sauce and bake for 8 minutes.

Makes three small pizzas

Ingredients

- ½ a batch of pizza dough
- 1 tbsp. olive oil
- 4-6 tbsps. tomato sauce
- 2 Cheddar cheese slices
- 3 tbsps. grated Cheddar cheese
- 3 thick slices Mozzarella cheese
- To decorate: Black and green olives, bell peppers

Heat oven to 375° F and grease a cookie sheet.

3 Remove from the oven, cool until safe to hold, then cut out the sun and moon shapes with kitchen scissors.

4 Cover the sun with cheese slices and the moon with grated Cheddar cheese. Cut out the spaceship and stars from Mozzarella.

5 Add the olives and peppers and bake for another 5 minutes.

Brown Tiger Pizza

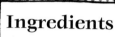

This brown tiger is made with whole wheat flour so it's really healthful.

Makes one tiger pizza

1 Shape the dough into three balls: one large ball for the tiger's face and two small balls for its ears.

2 Roll out the balls and push them together. Brush with olive oil and cover with grated cheese.

Push together

3 Use half slices of garlic sausage for the eyes, salami for the nose, mouth, and eyelids. Make whiskers and eyebrows with chives.

Ingredients

- ½ a batch of pizza dough made with whole wheat flour instead of white flour and 1 tsp. dried rosemary
- 1 tbsp. olive oil
- ½ cup grated Mozzarella or Cheddar cheese
- To decorate: 3 slices salami, 3 slices garlic sausage, chives, and black olives

Heat oven to 375° F and grease two cookie sheets.

4 Bake for 15–20 minutes.

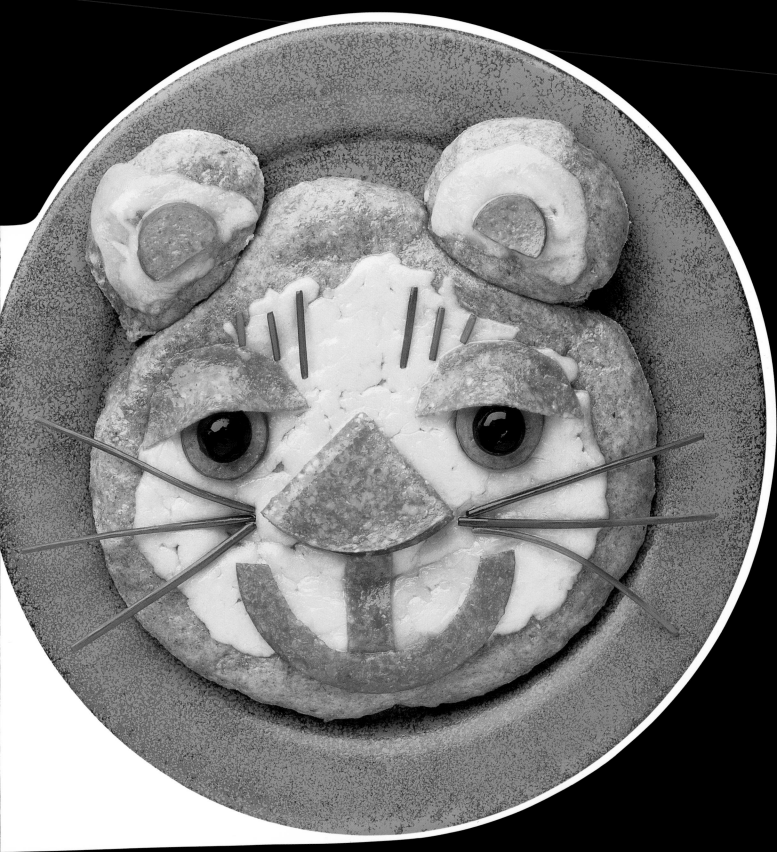

Baa Baa Pizza

This delicious green pizza is flavored with cheese, green onions, and spinach.

1 Knead the spinach, green onion, and Cheddar cheese into the risen dough.

2 Roll out the dough and brush it with olive oil.

3 Cut out the lamb from the Mozzarella cheese and the sun from the cheese slices. Use cut olives to make the lamb's legs, ear, eye, and nose.

Ingredients

- ½ a batch of pizza dough
- ½ cup chopped frozen spinach, thawed, drained, and patted dry
- 2 tbsps. chopped green onion
- ½ cup grated Cheddar cheese
- 1 tbsp. olive oil
- To decorate: 2 slices each of Mozzarella and Cheddar cheese, olives, bell peppers, cucumber

Heat the oven to 375° F and grease two cookie sheets.

cucumber stems

4 Bake for 15–20 minutes. Add the pepper flowers when cooked.

Cut flower shapes from pepper slices

14

Pizza Toadstool

You can make unusual pizzas simply by cutting the cooked dough into different shapes.

Makes one giant toadstool

1 Roll out the dough into a large circle, brush with olive oil, then cover the top half with mushrooms.

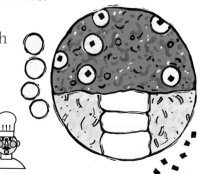

2 Sprinkle the whole pizza with grated Cheddar cheese, then add a thick layer of tomato sauce over the mushrooms.

3 Dot the tomato with smoked cheese buttons and tiny squares of olives, and arrange the Mozzarella slices below to make a stalk. Bake for 15–20 minutes.

4 When the pizza is cool enough to touch, cut out two triangles on either side of the Mozzarella to leave a stem.

Ingredients
- pizza dough
- 1 tbsp. olive oil
- 1 small can of sliced button mushrooms
- 4 tbsps. grated Cheddar cheese
- 4 tbsps. tomato sauce
- To decorate: 2 tiny rolls smoked cheese, black pitted olives
- 2 thick slices Mozzarella cheese

Heat oven to 375° F and grease a large cookie sheet.

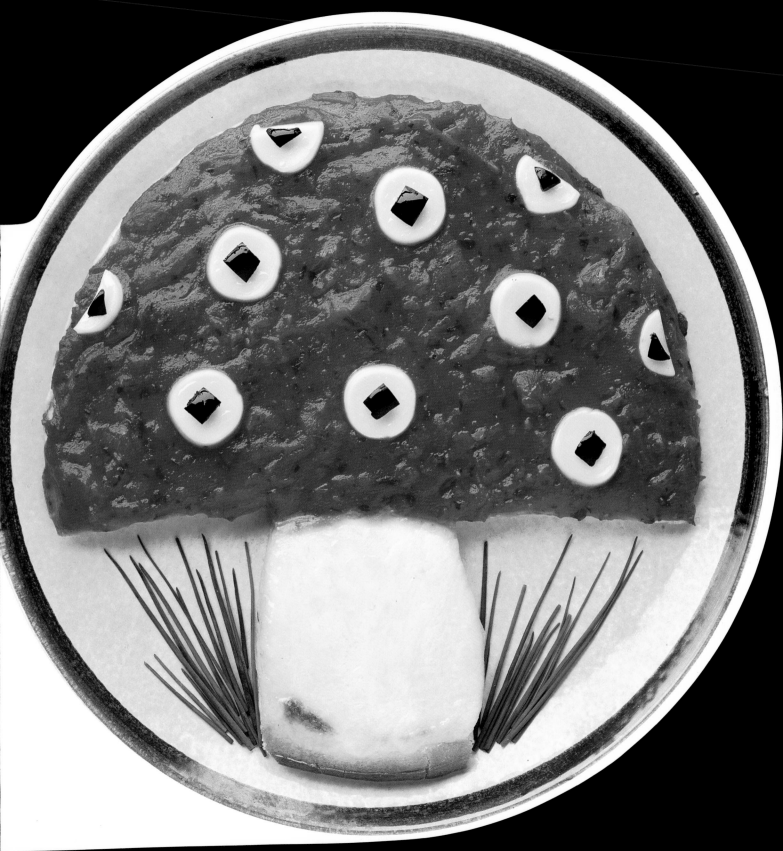

Pudgy Pete

Try making this tasty pizza, stuffed with cheese and pineapple.

Makes one very pudgy pizza

1 Divide the pizza dough into one large ball for the body, a medium-sized ball for the head, and four small balls for the hands and feet.

2 Stuff the body and head with ham, cheese, and pineapple. Flatten the balls a little with the palm of your hand and push them together.

Push together

3 Cover the legs with tomato sauce. Use cheese slices for the vest.

Add tomato-sauce cheeks

4 Make a face from a sliced olive, and use whole olives for buttons. Add a pepper tie and a cucumber belt.

Ingredients

- pizza dough
- 2 tbsps. chopped ham
- 3 tbsps. grated Cheddar cheese
- 2 tbsps. chopped pineapple
- 1 tbsp. olive oil
- 4 tbsps. tomato sauce
- To decorate: Cheese slices, olives, cucumber, bell peppers, small sprigs of broccoli

Heat oven to 375° F and grease a cookie sheet.

5 Bake for 15–20 minutes. Add small sprigs of broccoli hair when cool.

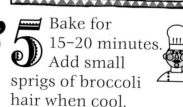

18

Snakey Stuffed Pizza

This snake is made from lots of tiny stuffed pizzas. Simply add more mini pizzas to make a longer snake!

Makes one long snake

1 Divide the dough into 13 balls for the snake's body and head, and stuff each ball with a little cheese and ham.

Push together

2 Arrange the balls in the shape of a snake on the cookie sheet. Brush the whole snake with olive oil.

3 Cover with tomato sauce. Decorate with cheese slices and shapes cut from peppers and pepperoni. Use olives for eyes.

4 Bake for 15–20 minutes. Remove from oven, make a hole at the front of the head with a toothpick, and add a tongue cut from red pepper.

Ingredients

- ½ a batch of pizza dough
- 4 tbsps. grated Cheddar cheese
- 4 tbsps. chopped ham
- 1 tbsp. olive oil
- 6 tbsps. tomato sauce
- 7 slices Mozzarella cheese
- To decorate: Pepperoni, bell peppers, olives

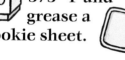

Heat oven to 375° F and grease a cookie sheet.

Cut shapes with tiny cookie cutters

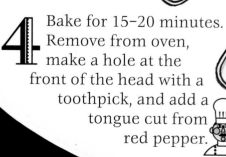

Pizza Snail

Pizzas don't have to be flat and round. Here, the pizza dough has been coiled and shaped to make a snail.

1 Divide the dough in half and knead the tomato paste into one half.

2 Roll out the other half with your hands, making a long sausage shape. Place the strips of salami over the top, then coil into a spiral.

Makes one pizza snail

Ingredients

- ½ a batch of pizza dough
- 2 tbsps. tomato paste
- 4 slices of salami, cut into strips
- 1 tbsp. olive oil
- 4 tbsps. tomato sauce
- To decorate: Pepperoni sticks, black pitted olives, bell peppers, salad leaves, parsley

Heat the oven to 375° F and grease a large cookie sheet.

Brush with olive oil

3 Shape the red dough into the snail's body, then press the body and shell together. Cover the body with tomato sauce, then add the pepperoni tentacles and an olive eye.

4 Bake for 15–20 minutes. Cut the peppers into butterfly shapes with cookie cutters. Serve on a bed of green salad.

pepper slices

Useful Words

Here are some special cooking words and abbreviations used in the recipes.

Chop – to cut into small pieces.

Spatula – a spreading tool with a long flat blade.

Grease – to rub a bowl or cookie sheet with a little oil so that dough doesn't stick to it.

Pitted – with the pits removed.

Sift – to shake flour through a strainer or flour sifter to remove any lumps.

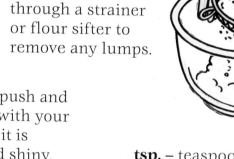

Knead – to push and pull dough with your hands until it is stretchy and shiny. To knead dough well, you should flatten it with the heel of your hand, fold it in half, then flatten it again. Keep doing this for about five minutes.

tsp. – teaspoon

tbsp. – tablespoon